Dec 2004

Kimberly ~

What a beautiful
    Child of God you are —
May you continually touch others
with the love of Christ —
        XO
    God Bless

Love Colleen.

Published by Barbour Publishing, Inc., P.O. Box 719, Uhrichsville, Ohio 44683, www.barbourbooks.com

Our mission is to publish and distribute inspirational products offering exceptional value and biblical encouragement to the masses.

Member of the
Evangelical Christian
Publishers Association

Printed in China
5 4 3 2 1

Let There Be Peace on Earth

Larissa Carrick

DayMaker
GREETING BOOKS

The
Prince of Peace
Is Born

For to us a child is born,
to us a son is given,
and the government will be on his shoulders.
And he will be called Wonderful Counselor,
Mighty God, Everlasting Father, Prince of Peace.
Of the increase of his government
and peace there will be no end.

ISAIAH 9:6–7

And the angel said unto them,

Fear not: for, behold,

I bring you good tidings of great joy,

which shall be to all people.

For unto you is born this day

in the city of David a Saviour,

which is Christ the Lord.

And this shall be a sign unto you;

Ye shall find the babe wrapped

in swaddling clothes,

lying in a manger.

And suddenly there was with the angel

a multitude of the heavenly host

praising God, and saying,

Glory to God in the highest,

and on earth peace,

good will toward men.

LUKE 2:10–14 KJV

Come worship the King! The Christ child is born!

peace

He brought **peace** on earth
and wants to bring it also into your **soul**—

that **peace** which the
world cannot give.
He is the **One** who would save

His **people** from their **sins.**

CORRIE TEN BOOM

Christ alone

can bring lasting **peace**—

peace with God—

peace among men and nations—

and **peace** within our hearts.

BILLY GRAHAM

Christ is the Morning Star...
who, when the night of
this world is past,
brings to His saints the promise of
the light of life and opens everlasting day.

VENERABLE BEDE

Christ had neither money, nor riches, nor earthly kingdom, for He gave the same to kings and princes. But He reserved one thing peculiarly to Himself, which no human creature or angel could do—namely, to conquer sin and death, the devil and hell, and in the midst of death to deliver and save those that through His Word believe in Him.

MARTIN LUTHER

When **Christ** came
into the **world**,
peace was sung;
and when **He**
went out of the world,
peace was bequested.

Francis Bacon

Peace, perfect peace,
in this dark world of sin?
The blood of Jesus
whispers peace within.

W. H. Bickersteth

8

peace

A great many people are
trying to make peace,
but that has already been done.
God has not left it for us to do;
all we have to do is enter into it.

DWIGHT L. MOODY

Be at peace with God

"Peace I leave with you; my peace I give you.
I do not give to you as the world gives.
Do not let your hearts be troubled
and do not be afraid."

JOHN 14:27

I will *lie* down
and sleep in **peace**,
for **you** alone,
O **LORD**,
make **me**
dwell in **safety**.

PSALM 4:8

peace

"Submit to God and be at **peace** with him;

in this way prosperity will come to you."

JOB 22:21

Peace does not mean

the end of all our **striving,**

Joy does not mean

the drying of our **tears.**

Peace is the **power**

that comes to **souls** arriving

Up to the **light** where

God Himself **appears.**

G. A. STUDDERT KENNEDY

Like a river glorious is God's perfect peace,
Over all victorious in its bright increase;
Perfect, yet it floweth fuller every day,
Perfect, yet it groweth deeper all the way.
Stayed upon Jehovah,
hearts are fully blest;
Finding, as He promised,
perfect peace and rest.

FRANCES RIDLEY HAVERGAL

Who except God can give you peace?
Has the world ever
been able to satisfy the heart?

ST. GERARD MAJELLA

peace

13

Great *peace* have they
who *love* your law,
and *nothing* can
make them *stumble.*

Psalm 119:165

God's *peace*. . .is far more wonderful than the human mind can understand. His *peace* will keep your thoughts and your hearts **quiet** and at **rest**.

PHILIPPIANS 4:7 TLB

Ask God for peace
and see what a transformation
will take place in your life.

BILLY GRAHAM

peace

He will give us **peace** in trouble.

When there is a **storm** without,

He will make **peace** within.

The world can create **trouble** in peace,

but **God** can create **peace** in trouble.

THOMAS WATSON

peace

Father,

I sometimes try to comfort myself with the ways of the world, to create my own peace through a false security. I often forget that the only true peace and security I will ever know comes from You. Your grace and forgiveness I sometimes take for granted, yet they are the most wonderful gifts a Father can give. Through You I am able to breathe freely, to let my heart rest in knowing that my life is in Your hands, and to be at peace. Thank You, Lord, for these precious gifts. They are undeserved, unsolicited, and often misunderstood. But I know that You love me, Lord, and You provide for me. I see evidence of this every minute of every day. My soul is at peace in Your love. Thank You for blessing me.

Amen.

Finding Peace
at Christmastime

Amidst the hustle and bustle,
remember the reason for the season,
the Christ child who was sent to earth
to save us all. . . .

When we celebrate Christmas we are celebrating that amazing time when the Word that shouted all the galaxies into being, limited all power, and for the love of us came to us in the powerless body of a human baby.

MADELINE L'ENGLE

peace

Let your **spirit** be blessed by the **grace**
our **Lord** grants and the **joy** He refreshes.
Take a deep **breath** and experience
the **wonder** of His **blessings!**

Christ is not only a

remedy for your weariness

and trouble, but He will

give you an abundance of

the contrary, **joy** and **delight.**

JONATHAN EDWARDS

peace

Do you remember
how to see Christmas
through the eyes of a child?

It's good to be **children** sometimes,

and never better than at **Christmas,**

when its mighty Founder

was a **child** Himself.

CHARLES DICKENS

peace

Try to remember when you were a child. . .when, in the days of tradition and togetherness, Christmas was the most exciting time of year. You were the first one awake on Christmas morning, unable to control your enthusiasm, running down the stairs to see what gifts were left for you under the tree. Did you get that toy you most wanted? Was there a wrapped package the size of the gift you were hoping for? Surely it was there somewhere. . .and you fought your way through a mountain of gifts, knowing in your heart that your parents had taken care of you, trusting that they had provided.

Now ask yourself, do you have the same kind of excitement in your heart today? Do you still have the same faith? God provides for us, not only on Christmas day, but every day. He gives us everything we need, including gifts that we don't even realize we need. We trust that He knows our hearts and loves us and that He will give us peace through our relationship with Him. Every day we receive His grace, His love, the security of knowing that He has better things in store. This Christmas, receive these gifts as a child would receive a new toy—with excitement, thanks, and, most of all, a joyful heart!

Father,

Sometimes I find myself feeling rather *un*-joyful during the Christmas season. I know I should be celebrating the birth of the Messiah, the one true God. I should be praising Him in every-thing I do, sharing His love with others, and doing good deeds to show my love for Him. Yet I find myself frustrated—waiting in lines, searching endlessly for the proper gift, reluctantly forcing myself to dish out batch after batch of snowman cookies, and worrying about finances. Please help me to focus on You—the reason for the season. For You are the hope in my heart, the love in my life, and the skip in my step. Help me to slow down and take time for myself, so that I may appreciate all of Your creation and so my heart can be at rest in relinquishing my control to You.

Amen.

peace peace peace peace peace peace peace peace

Share His Joy

Seek joy in what you give,
not in what you get.

AUTHOR UNKNOWN

To be simply ensconced
in God is true joy.

C. C. COLTON

Joy

Jesus
Others
Yourself

If you use the **joy** rule and think of **Jesus**,

then others, then yourself,

you will really feel **true joy**.

AUTHOR UNKNOWN

Real **joy** comes not from ease
or riches from praise of men,
but from **doing** something **worthwhile**.

Sir Wilfred Grenfell

Joy is the wine
that God is
ever pouring
Into the hearts of those
who strive with Him,
Lighting their eye
to vision and airing,
Strengthening their arms
to warfare glad and grim.

G. A. Studdert Kennedy

peace

Rejoicing is clearly a spiritual command. To ignore it is disobedience.

CHARLES SWINDOLL

The religion of Christ is the religion of joy. Christ came to take away our sins, to roll off our curse, to unbind our chains, to open our prison house, to cancel our debt; in a word, to give us the oil of joy for mourning, the garment of praise for the spirit of heaviness. Is not this joy? Where can we find a joy so real, so deep, so pure, so lasting? There is every element of joy—deep, ecstatic, satisfying, sanctifying joy—in the gospel of Christ. The believer in Jesus is essentially a happy man. The child of God is, from necessity, a joyful man. His sins are forgiven, his soul is justified, his person is adopted, his trials are blessings, his conflicts are victories, his death is immortality, his future is a heaven of inconceivable, unthought of, untold, and endless blessedness. With such a God, such a Savior, and such a hope, is he not, ought he not, to be a joyful man?

OCTAVIUS WINSLOW

Let There Be
Peace on Earth

But peace does not rest in the charters
and covenants alone.
It lies in the hearts and minds of all people.
So let us not rest all our hopes on parchment and on paper. . . .
Let us strive to build peace, a desire for peace,
a willingness to work for peace in the hearts
and minds of all of our people. I believe that we can.
I believe the problems of human destiny
are not beyond the reach of human beings.

JOHN F. KENNEDY

First keep the *peace* within yourself,

then you can also bring *peace* to others.

THOMAS À KEMPIS

We look forward to the *time*

when the power to *love* will replace the love of power.

Then will our world know the blessings of *peace*.

WILLIAM GLADSTONE

LORD, make me
an instrument of Thy

peace.

ST. FRANCIS OF ASSISI

Keep your heart in *peace;* let nothing in this world disturb it; everything has an end.

JOHN OF THE CROSS

peace reigns where our Lord reigns.

JULIAN OF NORWICH

Your life and my life flow into each other as wave flows into wave, and unless there is peace and joy and freedom for you, there can be no real peace or joy or freedom for me. To see reality—not as we expect it to be but as it is— is to see that unless we live for each other and in and through each other, we do not really live very satisfactorily; that there can really be life only where there really is, in just this sense, love.

FREDERICK BUECHNER, *THE MAGNIFICENT DEFEAT*

It isn't enough to talk about *peace.*

One must *believe* in it.

And it isn't enough to believe in it.

One must *work* at it.

ELEANOR ROOSEVELT

peace

Father,

Sometimes I feel that, with the turmoil in this world, a chance for peace seems unattainable. I try to live in my own little world and distance myself from the darkness, but I can only distance myself for so long. I have to believe that one person can make a difference, Lord. And I know how I can be that person. I will tell people of Your love. If I can share the gifts You've given me with just one person, over time, thousands could be affected for Your glory. The more people who have Your love in their hearts, the more who will know true peace. This Christmas, make me a messenger. Let me shout Your name from the hilltops! Let me show others what good Your Word has done in my life. May I carry Your peace with me always, Lord, and may I make a difference in this world—for You. In Thy name, I pray with all of my heart.

Amen.